JAMES STEVENSON

THE MOST AMAZING DINOSAUR

Greenwillow Books *An Imprint of* HarperCollins*Publishers*

Watercolor paints and a black pen
were used for the full-color art.
The text type is Kuenstler 480 BT.

The Most Amazing Dinosaur
Copyright © 2000
by James Stevenson
Printed in Singapore
by Tien Wah Press.
All rights reserved.
http://harperchildrens.com

Library of Congress
Cataloging-in-Publication Data

Stevenson, James (date)
The most amazing dinosaur /
by James Stevenson.
    p.   cm.
"Greenwillow Books."
Summary: Wilfred the rat stumbles
into a museum, where he befriends
the animals living there and enjoys
the many exhibits.
ISBN 0-688-16432-3 (trade).
ISBN 0-688-16433-1 (lib. bdg.)
[1. Museums—Fiction.
2. Rats—Fiction.
3. Animals—Fiction.]
I. Title.
PZ7.S84748Mi   2000
[E]—dc21   99-25347   CIP

10 9 8 7 6 5 4 3 2 1
First Edition

Wilfred had been on the road a long time.

As night came, a cold wind began to wail.

Wilfred pedaled faster on his old bike, trying
to keep warm.

"No friends, no food, nowhere to sleep," said Wilfred.

"Oh, well—at least it isn't raining."

Just then a large snowflake floated by. Then another,
and another.

"Oh-oh," said Wilfred.

He came to an enormous stone building
with big stairs and towers.

"I'll bet it's toasty in there," said Wilfred.
"Just the place for a wet rat to catch some shut-eye."
He knocked at a door, but nobody answered.

"Maybe there's an open window someplace,"
said Wilfred. He climbed up a drainpipe.

No windows were
open anywhere.

Wilfred sat on a chimney
and wondered what to do next.

A gust of wind came along,
and he fell into the chimney.

Wilfred tumbled down through the darkness
and landed in a cloud of soot.

He walked across the room,
leaving footprints of soot on the rug.

He went out the door
into a hallway.

"Got to find a place to sleep,"
said Wilfred. "Maybe in here . . ."

He turned a corner.
A giant skeleton was standing there.
"Ooops!" said Wilfred. "Wrong place!"

He hurried on. There were skeletons everywhere.
Wilfred ran faster and faster until . . .

he crashed into something soft. It was an owl.

"I beg your pardon?" said the owl. "Where do you think you're going?"

"Sorry," said Wilfred. "I got spooked by all these skeletons."

"Haven't you ever been to a museum before?" said the owl.

"Is that what this is?" said Wilfred.

"Yes," said the owl.

"To tell you the truth," said Wilfred, "this is my first museum."

"Welcome," said the owl. "My name is Prichett." "I'm Wilfred," said Wilfred. "Is there any place here I could get some sleep?" "Millions of places," said Prichett. "Just don't get caught."

A snail peeked out from under an elephant.
"Good evening, Prichett," said the snail.
"Hello, Harry," said Prichett.
"This is Wilfred. He'll be staying for the night."
"Sleep well," said Harry.

"Hi, Prichett," called a squirrel from on top
of a huge whale.
"Hi, Leo," called Prichett. "Say hello to Wilfred.
He's new here!"
"Howdy, Wilf," said Leo. "Enjoy the museum!"

Suddenly Prichett and Wilfred saw a flashlight coming.
"I know you are here," called a voice.
"It's Mr. Thrawl, the head of the museum!"
whispered Prichett. "If he catches us, he'll throw us
out in the snow!"

"Somebody is in my museum!" called Mr. Thrawl.
"I saw his footprints on my nice, clean rug."
"That would be me," whispered Wilfred to Prichett.
"Hide!" said Prichett, and flew away.

Wilfred opened a small door and ducked in.
It was dark and quiet, and the floor felt like
squishy moss. "Very nice," said Wilfred.
He stretched out, leaning against
what might have been a tree.
In a moment
he was sound
asleep.

When Wilfred woke up, he was on a mountain with a family of gorillas. "I'll be darned," he said.

He went out the little door and ran into a skunk.

"How was Africa?" said the skunk.

"Great!" said Wilfred. "Where do you sleep?"

"The South Pole," said the skunk.

"By the way, my name is Buxton."

"I'm Wilfred," said Wilfred.

"Are you hungry?" said Buxton.

"Extremely," said Wilfred.

"Follow me," said Buxton.
They went down to the cellar of the museum.

They crawled under a lot of pipes.
"It's not much farther," said Buxton.
"Up these stairs!"

They climbed through a trap door.
"Where are we?" said Wilfred.
"The cafeteria," said Buxton.
"Grab a tray!"

Buxton and Wilfred helped themselves to sandwiches,
pies, cakes, doughnuts, and ice cream.
Then Buxton looked at the clock. "Oh-oh," he said.
"It's almost time to open. Let's get out of here!"
They went down through the trap door just as
the cooks arrived.

"Let's go see Prichett," said Wilfred.

"Where does he hang out?"

"Up in the attic," said Buxton.

"Welcome to *my* museum," said Prichett.

"Come on in—it's free!"

"What's in here?" said Wilfred.
"Bottle caps, acorns, dried leaves,
lost mittens and toys,"
said Prichett.
"Nice exhibit,"
said Buxton.

"How did you build this dinosaur?" said Wilfred.
"I made it from old ice cream sticks," said Prichett.
"Amazing," said Wilfred.
"Come on, Wilfred," said Buxton. "There's a lot
more to see!"

That night Wilfred and his new friends played hide-and-seek in the big museum.

Harry hid in the shell collection.

Leo hid in the jungle.

Prichett hid with the birds in the marsh.

Wilfred tried to hide in the fish collection, but everyone spotted him right away.

Suddenly Leo called, "Mr. Thrawl
is coming! Mr. Thrawl is coming!"
Everybody quickly climbed up
on a dinosaur. Mr. Thrawl
marched past down below.
They could hear him
talking to himself.
"Everything must be perfect
when the inspectors come,"
he was saying. "Perfect,
perfect, perfect . . ."

Just then Leo leaned out to peek . . .
and fell off his bone.

He crashed
down on Wilfred,
and they both
fell on Buxton.
Then Leo and Wilfred
and Buxton hit Prichett
and Harry, and they all
tumbled to the floor.

The entire dinosaur fell apart and
collapsed in a cloud of dust.

Mr. Thrawl crawled out from under the pile.
"Oh, no!" he said. "When the inspectors
see this, I will lose my job."

Then he saw Wilfred and the others.
"Get out!" he cried. "Get out of this museum
immediately! You have wrecked my career!"

That night Wilfred and the others sat in the park across the street from the museum. The snow fell all around them. Harry sneezed. "Cold out here," he said. "For snails, I mean." Wilfred picked up Harry and put him in his pocket. "Thanks, Wilfred," said Harry, from inside. "This is nice."

"I feel sorry for old Thrawl," said Leo. "It wasn't his fault the dinosaur fell down."
"It was our fault," said Prichett. "I sort of wish we could help him."

The next morning Mr. Thrawl met the museum inspectors at the front door.

"Let's see the dinosaur room first," said one of the inspectors.

"What's the rush?" said Mr. Thrawl. "They certainly aren't going anywhere."

"We aren't here to dilly-dally," said an inspector.

"Open the door to the dinosaurs."

"Well, what do you know?" said Mr. Thrawl.

"The darn door seems to be locked."

"Let me try," said an inspector.

The door swung open.

Mr. Thrawl gasped. A giant dinosaur was standing on one leg.
"Astonishing!" said an inspector. "I've never seen one like it!"
"Neither have I!" said Mr. Thrawl.
"Congratulations, Mr. Thrawl," said an inspector.
"Very impressive!"

"I imagine you had a lot of help on this project," said
another inspector.
"I imagine I did," said Mr. Thrawl. "I mean yes, I did."
Prichett and Harry and Leo and Buxton and Wilfred stood
smiling and waving from a windowsill across the room.

When the inspectors left,
they told Mr. Thrawl his
museum was the best
they had ever inspected.

Mr. Thrawl found Prichett and Wilfred and
the others sitting on the museum steps.
"Come in, come in!" he called. "I want to
hire you all as my special assistants!"

"Could we live in the museum?" said Prichett.
"And eat in the cafeteria?" said Buxton.
"Yes, to everything!" said Mr. Thrawl.

That winter Prichett worked on the exhibits,

Buxton served meals,

Harry cleaned display cases,

and Wilfred and Leo repaired the roofs.

When spring came, Wilfred said good-bye to his friends and got on his bike.

"I want to see real elephants and penguins and bears and whales," he said. "After that, I'll be back!"

"I want to see those things, too," said a voice from his pocket. "Mind if I tag along?"

"Always room for one more, Harry," said Wilfred, and they rode off together.